A NEXT GENERATION NOVEL

PROMISE
Us

J.M. WALKER

IBSN: 978-1-989782-47-7

FAMILY TREE

Angel and Genevieve "Jay" Rodriguez
(Grit, King's Harlots #1/Grim, King's Harlots #3)
Angelica "Gigi"
Ryder
Meadow

Asher and Meeka Donovan
(Stain, King's Harlots #2)
Aiden
Ashton

Coby and Brogan Porter
(Rude, King's Harlots #4/For You, King's Harlots #7)
Zachary "Zach"

Dale and Maxine "Max" Michaels
(Numb, King's Harlots #5)
Piper

Vincent "Stone" and Creena Stone
(Rust, King's Harlots #6)
Luna
Vincent Junior

Greyson and Eve Mercer
(Greyson, Hell's Harlem #1)
Jaron

Tray and Zillah Lister
(Tray, Hell's Harlem #2)
Beatrix "Bee"

John and Beatrix "Trixie" Butcher
(Hell's Harlem Series)
Cyrus
Samson "Sammy"

PART ONE

ONE

RYDER

I SAW HER STRUGGLING.

The beautiful woman had her arms full, with a box in one arm and two bags in her other hand.

Her long blonde hair was pulled back into a ponytail. She had a light tan and I found myself wondering if she had freckles from when the sun kissed her skin. She was heading to a small white sports car. I assumed it was her vehicle. Especially after she placed the box and bags into the back seat, shut the door, and ran her hand over the sleek edge of the roof. Maybe she had saved up for it and it took so long for her to get it, and now that she finally had it, she was grateful. Or maybe, it was a gift from someone she loved who had passed. Or her husband bought it for her.

My stomach clenched at that last thought. My chest tightened as a sour taste filled my mouth. For whatever reason, the thought that another man had put a ring on her finger didn't sit well with me.

I was about to head home after finishing up with some construction at The Dove Project but now that I saw this woman, I thought better of it. She looked familiar though. I must have seen her around the center before.

The Dove Project had been in the family long before I was ever born. My mom, along with my friends' mothers, created the center to help those in need. Victims of abuse and human trafficking could come for safety and shelter. And a shit ton of food too. My sister, Meadow, baked and she baked a lot. I wasn't sure she actually knew how to bake for only a handful of people. But she loved it. Every time I saw her small form disappearing into the kitchen, I couldn't help but notice the light in her eyes and the smile on her face. I wondered if she even knew how happy baking made her. She was a good cook too, but baking was her calling.

A hard sigh pulled me from my thoughts.

The woman was leaning against the side of her car, glancing down at the cell phone in her hand. Her brow was pinched in the middle, her cheeks a mottled pink.

Before I could stop myself, I took a step toward her until I was only a few feet away. "Everything okay?"

She jumped, her head snapping up. Her frown deepened when her beautiful blue eyes landed on me. "Excuse me?"

I coughed, my face heating. "I mean...fuck, I suck at this shit."

Her face softened, a laugh bubbling from her. She stuck her phone in her back pocket before turning toward me. "What shit is that?"

"I saw you struggling with the box and bags and was going to come help you but got distracted," I confessed, surprised at how easy it was to talk to her.

"What did you get distracted by?" she asked, raising an eyebrow.

"Uh..." I smirked. "I was distracted by how beautiful you are."

She blinked. Once. Twice. Before her face broke out into a huge grin. A laugh followed. "That was slick."

I shrugged. "It did want I wanted."

"Oh? And what was that?"

"It made you smile." I winked.

She shook her head, that same smile staying on her lips. "I've seen you around here before."

"My sisters volunteer here. Meadow bakes and Gigi helps in other areas. She's a dancer and sometimes holds classes for the girls here too." I stood up taller, proud of my sisters and the career paths they had chosen.

"Oh yes." My beautiful new obsession, beamed. "I know them. Gigi's invited me to a few of the parties she used to throw but I've been so busy with school that I haven't had a chance to ever go. And I'm also not overly good with crowds or people I don't know."

"You seem fine with me," I corrected her.

"Yeah." The woman took a step toward me, letting her eyes roam down the length of me. "That's because it's just you and me."

My body stirred. *Interesting.* "What's your name, beautiful?"

Her eyes snapped to mine, that delicious flush in her cheeks darkening. "Clara." She stuck out her hand. "Clara Blanco."

I wrapped my fingers around hers, giving her a gentle tug until she was another step closer and kissed the back of her hand. "My name's Ryder. Ryder Rodriguez." Letting my lips linger a little longer than deemed necessary, I watched as that flush in her cheeks slid all the way down into the V of her white t-shirt.

"You are a slick one, aren't you, handsome?" she murmured, licking her full, ruby red lips.

"Nah." I rose to my full height, released her hand, and shoved mine into my pockets. "I'm leaving on Monday, saw you, made a mission to approach you and here we are."

"Where are you going on Monday?" she asked, crossing her arms under her chest.

"I'm in the military, Clara," I said gently.

3

Her eyes brightened. "My granddaddy was a sergeant. He died doing something secretive. I don't know what. No one ever told us. Or if they do know, they never told us kids anyway."

I nodded. "Understandable."

"So, what do you do in the military, Ryder?" Clara asked.

"Stuff that I can't talk about." Truth was, I shot up the ranks rather quickly. My father was impressed. He had told me on more than one occasion how proud he was of me. He had also said that I was a faster learner than him.

"Oh." Clara turned away from me. "Well, it was nice meeting you, Ryder."

"Wait." I closed the distance between us and gently grabbed her upper arm. "It's not because I don't want to tell you. Trust me. I do. I want to tell so many people, but I'm not allowed. It's for everyone who's involved, my career, my life. It's to keep people safe. The less you know, the better."

She searched my face. Probably deciding if I was telling the truth or not. Most cases, I wouldn't care if the person believed me but there was something about Clara that called out to me. I liked her. Even though I had just found out her name, I had seen her around the center before. She cared for people and had a big heart. That was a bonus in my books. It was one of the reasons why I decided to join the military in the first place. Besides wanting to follow in my father's footsteps, I wanted to fight for our country. Our ancestors fought for our freedom and I wanted to continue that fight for the generations to come.

"Okay." She pursed her lips. "Well, that's fair." She faced me, giving me her full undivided attention. "So, Ryder. What do you have planned for your weekend before you have to leave?"

"I'm having dinner at my parents' place tomorrow night with my sisters and some friends. Sunday will be spent reassuring my mother that I'll be coming home again." Even though I knew it was a possibility that I wouldn't, I had to tell her different. It was the only way she would let me leave.

"What about tonight?" Clara asked, pulling her phone from her back pocket.

"Tonight, I hope to be spending it with a woman."

"Oh?" Clara raised a perfect blonde eyebrow. "Is she pretty?"

"No." I took a step toward her. "She's absolutely breathtaking."

Her cheeks reddened, a slow grin spreading on her face. "Are you asking me on a date, Ryder?"

My body stirred. Fuck me, I loved when she said my name and if I had it my way, she'd be screaming it by morning.

I wasn't the type of guy who had one-night stands. I would rather be abstinent than sleep around. It just wasn't my thing. But even if sex didn't happen tonight with Clara, I knew from the moment I saw her, before I even knew her name, that I wanted to spend tonight with her.

Clara handed me her phone. "Type in your number."

I smirked, taking the phone from her and texting my cell instead. "I sent myself a text." I handed the phone back to her.

Taking a chance, I pushed a strand of hair behind her ear. "Text me your address. I'll pick you up at eight tonight." I took a step away from her. "Oh, and make sure you wear a sweater." She wouldn't need it, but I was being a gentleman by reminding her. I had plans of being the only thing to warm her up.

Before she could respond, I was jogging to my truck with a wide smile on my face.

TWO

Clara

I HAD NO IDEA what the hell just happened.

I knew Meadow and Gigi had a brother, but I had never met him. Not officially anyway. And I didn't remember him looking like *that*. Tall. Dark eyes. Tanned skin. And big. He was wide in the shoulders and I knew that if he ever hugged me, I would feel safe, enveloped in his large frame.

As soon as I sat in my car, I checked my phone. Ryder had done what he said and texted me. I sent him my address, drove home and stewed the whole way about what I was going to wear. I still had a few hours before he would pick me up, but I knew that by the time eight rolled around, I'd still probably be wondering what I should wear.

Should I just be comfortable?

Sexy?

In between?

I had no idea.

When I parked the car, I took a breath and looked out at the three-story walk-up I lived in. The rent was cheap, the location wasn't too bad, and the other residents were nice.

A soft tap on the window made me jump.

Frank, another resident who lived on the main floor of the building, gave me one of his genuine wide smiles.

Killing the engine, I left the car and shut the door behind me. "Frank, how are you?"

"Good." He searched my face. "I was out for my afternoon walk and saw you pull in and sit there for a few minutes. Thought something was wrong. So came to check on you."

My heart warmed. "Thank you. I'm fine though. I have a date tonight and I'm nervous."

Frank's eyes lit up. "That's fun!"

I laughed. "Yes, but it's been a while." It wasn't like I had guys lined up at the door to take me out on the town or anything.

"You will have fun and if the guy hurts you, I'll kill him." Frank shrugged. "So, it's a win-win really."

I shook my head. "He's sweet. And he's leaving on Monday. He's in the military."

Frank stood taller at the mention of the forces. "Do you know what he does?"

"No. It's all hush-hush I guess," I told him. "But he's nice." He had to be nice since he was in the military, right?

"Just be careful, sweetheart." Frank started walking away. "Remember what I said."

"I'll remember." I grabbed the bags from the back seat before kicking the door closed. "Thank you," I called after him and rushed to the building.

It was pushing four in the afternoon. I wondered why Ryder set the date so late. Not that eight was overly late but I hadn't eaten much during the day.

I sighed. I was stressing. I didn't like stressing.

Taking a breath, I mentally counted to ten and headed up the stairs to my floor.

When I finally reached my apartment, I shut the door behind me, clicked the lock into place, and began stripping. Gathering my clothes, I went to my bedroom and changed into workout clothes. Maybe doing a round of yoga for an hour would help me feel better. No. Punching something would probably be better but unfortunately for me, I had nothing to hit. Not safely anyway. There was a gym at the center I volunteered at but I never had the courage to actually work out in it.

After doing a hard round of yoga, I took a shower, did my hair. and the next thing I knew, it was pushing seven. I was standing in front of my closet in a towel. At least I was showered.

With a glass of red wine in my hand, I went through my closet and hated everything I owned. Who needs eight black dresses? This girl apparently. And black leggings? Way too many.

Taking a step back, I began pacing when something caught my eye.

A dress that I couldn't remember when I last wore it, hung in the middle of the closet. It was black with tiny red polka dots on it. It buttoned up the middle and would sit just past my knees. It was short-sleeved, classy, and the comfiest dress I had ever worn. I could sex it up a bit and wear something hot beneath it.

Happy with my choice, I pulled the dress off the hanger and laid it on my bed. Ripping off the towel, I grabbed a red bra and panty set from my drawer.

Finally getting dressed, I did a quick turn in the mirror and unbuttoned the top two buttons of the dress. It showed off some cleavage but left enough to the imagination that I wouldn't feel like Ryder was staring at my tits the whole time. Or maybe I would be lucky, and he was an ass man instead.

I sighed, applied some lip gloss, and gave myself another once-over. It would have to do.

My phone dinged, indicating a new text message.

Ryder: I'm here.

I smiled, my heart speeding up.

Me: On my way down.

Grabbing my small purse, I threw my phone in it and slipped my feet into a pair of wedges.

Locking up the apartment, I quickly made my way downstairs. As soon as I stepped outside, I was thankful with my choice of outfit. It was a warmer evening. I was almost tempted to throw my hair up into a ponytail but when I caught Ryder standing by his truck, his dark eyes on me, I changed my mind.

A slow grin spread on his face the closer I got to him. "You look beautiful."

My cheeks heated. "You look handsome."

"Ready?" he asked, opening the passenger door to his black truck.

I took a breath and nodded. "I am." But it didn't mean I wasn't nervous.

He stepped to the side, letting me enter the vehicle and helping me up onto the seat.

When I was inside the truck, I turned to him. "Thank you."

Ryder winked, closed the door, and headed around the vehicle to the driver's side door. Once he was sitting beside me, he turned on the engine and pulled us out of the driveway.

"How was your afternoon?" I asked, needing the sound of our voices to drown out the nerves rushing through my belly.

"Not too bad." He passed a glance at me. "Took me forever to figure out what I wanted to wear. I tried asking my sisters, but they were no help."

I laughed. "Really? You had a hard time deciding too?"

He chuckled. "Yeah, babe. Believe it or not, guys can get nervous too."

"Oh." I wiped my sweaty palms on my thighs. "I knew that, but I just never had a guy be nervous when it comes to going on a date with me."

"How come?" Ryder grabbed my hand, holding it tight in his.

That single touch eased the nerves racing through me. "I haven't dated the best guys. Or the guys I was supposed to date ended up being in love with someone else." I grimaced at the memory rushing through me.

"Explain that part to me."

I thought a moment. "You actually may know them. Ashton and Aidan Donovan."

Ryder grunted. "I do. And Zach and Luna. I know them all."

"I forgot you all grew up together." I was an outsider looking in. "Ashton set me up on a date with Zach, but never told me that Zach had said no because he was in love with Luna. It was a hot mess but I like to think I gained a friend out of it." Zach, Luna, and I had gone on several dinner dates together. Even though it had only been the three of us, they never made me feel like a third wheel.

"I heard something about that. My sister, Meadow, likes to keep me in the loop." Ryder chuckled, his big body shaking.

I laughed. "Yeah. If you want to know something, just go to her. But she doesn't spread shit. She says it how it is. I can appreciate that," I told him.

"Are you close with my sisters?"

"Not really. I'm not close with anyone." I wasn't sad about that either. I was focused on school and my career. Much like Ryder and his need to serve our country, I had a need to save children from monsters.

"Well." Ryder brought our joined hands up to his mouth. "You can become close with me."

My heart stuttered.

He placed a soft peck on my knuckles, winked, and dropped my hand back on my lap.

My stomach somersaulted. Oh yeah, I could definitely see myself becoming close with him.

"So, tell me, Ryder. Why did you really ask me out on a date? Did you want to sow some oats before being shipped away?"

His jaw clenched, a gruff laugh leaving him. "I'm not like any of the guys you've ever dated, Clara. If that's what you're wondering."

"Oh? And how do you know what the guys I've dated were like?" I turned toward him, linking my fingers in his. "You only just met me today. Officially anyway. You ask me out on a date and then tell me that you're leaving on Monday. Why me? What makes me so special?" I didn't want to second-guess his motives but after having some bad luck with guys and being considered a second choice, it made me question…well, everything when it came to dating and the opposite sex.

"Who the fuck hurt you, baby?"

I let go of his hand and crossed my arms under my chest. "It doesn't matter."

"Well, it must matter enough for you to question my motives." He sighed. "Listen, I saw you. I watched you for a few minutes before I actually got the balls to approach you. Yes, I'm shipping out on Monday, but I won't be gone forever. I wanted to go on this date and see where things went. I'm not looking for a random fuck. I want to get to know you, Clara. That's it. If after tonight, you just want to be friends, that's fine too. You just let me know."

"I'm sorry." The back of my neck heated. "I've had some bad luck with guys, and I guess you asking me out on a date surprised me."

Ryder leaned an elbow on the windowsill, scratching his jaw. "I get that. I don't date a lot. I won't lie and say that I've never had a one-night stand. I'm not home a lot, so it's hard to keep a relationship. I have to do what I can to take the edge off. But if we're both happy with how tonight goes, that ends. I promise you. I'm not a cheater or a player. I know the twins tried setting you up with Zach."

"Yeah, that backfired and was embarrassing," I mumbled.

"I'm sorry that happened to you but I like to think it actually worked out in my favor."

I looked at Ryder.

He winked, waggling his eyebrows.

I laughed, the heaviness in the air, dissipating. "I'm glad it didn't work out. I like Luna. I wouldn't want anything to ruin what little friendship I have there. I don't really hang out with the girls, but I do like them."

He gave me a small smile. "How's school going?"

"It's hard but I'm determined," I said honestly, thankful for the change in subject. "I'm more of a hands-on kind of person. It's the in-class shit that stresses me out."

"I get that."

"Where are we going?" I asked when I realized that we were no longer in town.

"You'll see." Ryder winked.

That small movement sent a nervous flutter racing through me. Nervous because I knew that I could fall for him and dangerously so. He was different. Raised well. Good head on his shoulders. And he had a single mission on his mind and that was to fight for his country.

Ten minutes later and we were pulling down a gravel road.

"Nervous?" Ryder asked.

"Yeah, I'm wondering if you're going to leave me out here by myself." I sat forward, seeing a clearing at the end of the road. It overlooked...my eyes widened. "Wow."

He chuckled. "Beautiful, isn't it?"

"It is." I had heard of a stunning view that overlooked our town, but no one had ever brought me here.

Once we reached the edge of the cliff, Ryder turned the truck around and backed it up. "We'll be able to watch the sunset from here."

My heart warmed that he had thought of that. I wasn't overly girly, but I did enjoy dressing up from time to time and just being treated like a queen. What female didn't? It had always been the little things that mattered most to me.

Ryder killed the engine and slipped from the truck. "Coming?" he asked before shutting the door.

I took a breath and left the vehicle, not overly sure what I had gotten myself into but excited to see where this night went just the same.

Much to my surprise, Ryder started rolling back the cover on the bed of his truck. When he was done, I just stood there, staring at what laid before me.

He chuckled. "Surprised?"

"Uh...I really have no...I just..." My heart warmed and I think I swooned a little bit.

Ryder came toward me, a satisfied smile sitting on his face. "Did I do okay?" He took my hand, bringing it up to his mouth.

I nodded, chewing my bottom lip.

He winked. "I think we should test it out." He kept hold of my hand and helped me up into the bed of the truck. I kicked off my wedges and sank my toes into the plush feather bed. There were two pillows sitting at the head of it. A bucket with a bottle of wine and two bottles of water sat to my right.

Ryder snapped two ends of wires together and a row of lights that sat around the edge of the bed turned on.

It was beautiful, romantic, and damn near perfect. No. Correction. It *was* perfect. No other guy had ever done this for me before.

"Do you like it, Clara?" Ryder asked, his brow scrunching in the middle.

"Oh God." I shook my head, my eyes welling. "Yes. I can't...I have no words."

He joined me in the back of the truck and sat beside me. "I didn't mean..." He reached out, wiping a tear that had fallen down my cheek.

"Oh..." I laughed, my face heating. "I'm such a romantic but no one has ever done this for me before. Thank you, Ryder. I really have no words."

His grin grew, his shoulders dropping with relief. "I'm glad you like it, but I can't take full credit. Gigi came across a picture on Facebook and both her and Meadow gave me ideas."

"You planned this all today?" I asked, taken aback that he would be so damn considerate and do this with such short notice.

He nodded slowly. "I wanted to impress you. I know we don't know each other and it's hard to trust anyone these days. But thank you for putting your trust in me and letting me take you out tonight."

I leaned forward and placed a soft peck on his cheek. "Thank you for this."

"I told the center where you are, so if you end up feeling uncomfortable and want to leave, someone can pick you up."

As if on cue, my phone dinged. I pulled it from my purse and found a text from... "It's your mom." I looked up at Ryder.

Jay: I know you're out with my son tonight and that you don't know each other really but if you need anything, you don't hesitate to call me. Understand?

Me: Yes, ma'am.

Jay: And don't call me ma'am.

Jay Rodriguez had set up The Dove Project with friends years ago. It was a place for victims of human trafficking and domestic violence and more. I had been volunteering there for the past few years. It also looked good on my college application. Ryder's mom had been nothing but supportive.

"I can't believe you did this," I said to Ryder. "You told your mom where I was in case I didn't feel safe?"

Ryder shrugged. "Why not? I like you, Clara. I wouldn't have asked you out if I didn't. And I know a lot of people don't start dating until they actually know each other. But when I saw you today, I wanted more. Do I know exactly what that is? No. I need to focus on my career."

"Me too." I looked down at my lap, picking at a random fuzz on my dress. "But for one night, I don't want to think about school or careers."

A wide grin spread on his face. "Good. Because neither do I." He leaned forward and pulled the bottle of wine from the bucket. "Did you want a glass?"

THREE

RYDER

I NEVER EXPECTED MY romantic gesture to actually bring out any sort of emotion in Clara. My sisters had been right in saying she would love it. Unless she was a good fucking actor and was just saying she loved the surprise to make me feel better about myself.

I chanced a glance at her.

She sighed every so often, a small smile splaying on her face as she sipped her wine.

Nope. She definitely loved the surprise.

"So, tell me, Clara." I reached out, brushing my thumb along the back of her arm, my cock jerking at the tiny goosebumps dancing along her skin. "What would you have been doing tonight if I hadn't taken you out?"

She barked a laugh. "Drinking wine by myself and watching Netflix." She turned toward me. "I live a very exciting life."

"Sounds like it," I teased. "Well, if it makes you feel any better, my life is even more exciting. I would be babysitting my nephew or better yet, hanging out by myself. But drinking beer instead."

Clara giggled. "Would you be watching Netflix too?"

I scoffed. "Of course." I tapped her nose. "What else is there to watch?"

She licked her lips. "Porn."

I grinned. "Porn doesn't really do it for me. I'd rather the real stuff." I glanced down at her mouth, itching to have a taste. Even just a small one. Could she feel this connection? Was it just me? Maybe it was all in my head. Either way, I wanted her. We didn't have to do anything tonight, but I did want to spend the night with her. Even if it was just to talk.

"Interesting." Clara took a sip of her wine. "Anything on Netflix you're currently obsessed with?"

We spent the next hour or so discussing our favorite shows and eating the assortment of cheese and crackers I had packed. It wasn't a full course meal, but Clara seemed to appreciate the food. We also talked about what we could watch over and over again. I learned that she loved zombies and was hooked on *The Walking Dead*. I had also come to understand that she looked forward to finishing school but that was all she would say about it. She closed up rather quickly when I asked her about her career choice. She was going to be a social worker. I couldn't imagine that would be easy but volunteering at The Dove Project would definitely give her some experience.

"Oh, I'm out of wine." Clara pouted, a rosy glow hitting her cheeks.

"Actually." I reached into a bag and pulled out another bottle. "I didn't want you thinking I was taking advantage of you or anything, so I kept this hidden until you asked for it."

"Well, aren't you sweet." She grabbed the bottle from me and twisted off the cap. "Cheers." She clinked it against my glass and took a sip right from the bottle itself.

I chuckled. "So classy."

She laughed, shrugged, and took another sip.

Before she could get drunk on me, I grabbed the bottle from her, took a sip of my own and put the cap back on it.

"Ryder." She reached for the bottle.

"No." I put it away and cupped her cheek. "I want…"

"What?" she breathed, her eyes darkening. "You want to kiss me?"

"I want to do more than that, but a kiss is a good start," I told her, my voice low.

"Well, then I think you should kiss me, and we can go from there."

Moving my hand to the back of her head, I tilted it back, giving me access to her throat. "You know." I kissed her neck, licking up the length of it to her jaw. "I wasn't planning on doing this. I wanted to take it slow. I was trying to be a gentleman for you. But you're beautiful, sassy, and so fucking hot."

"Ryder," she whispered, her chest rising and falling.

Taking a chance, I kept my hand fisted in her hair and stared at her. "You tell me to stop and I'll stop. You hear me?"

She nodded. "I won't tell you to stop."

We had finished off a bottle of wine, but I wasn't feeling any sort of buzz. I searched her face. Her eyes were clear. A rosy glow was on her cheeks, but I had quickly realized that she blushed even before we got into the wine. "Say it, Clara."

"If I say stop, you'll stop. I got it." She reached up and started unbuttoning the top few buttons on her dress. "But trust me, Ryder. I won't say it."

My eyes fell to her chest.

Her fingers worked over the tiny buttons. When she reached to just below her chest, she pulled the fabric apart, revealing a red lace bra. It pushed her tits up, giving me a view of her perfect chest.

"Clara."

We shouldn't be doing this and so soon, but as much as I was thinking about it, I couldn't voice the thoughts rushing through me. Truth was, I wanted to go away with some happy memories.

19

"Is something wrong?" She pulled away from me, a dark shadow passing over her face. When she went to do up the buttons, I covered her hands, stopping her.

"No. Nothing's wrong. I just..." I took a breath, the back of my neck heating. "I want this. I want you. But I don't want you thinking that I'm using you."

She gave me a small smile and laid down. "Trust me. If I was worried about that, I wouldn't be here."

"I'm leaving on Monday," I reminded her.

"I know." She grabbed onto the collar of my shirt and pulled me down until I was mere inches from her mouth. "Let me give you a going away present."

FOUR

Clara

I COULD SENSE THAT Ryder was closing in on himself. I appreciated that he was thinking of me, but it had been so long, and I knew there was a connection between us. I could feel it and I knew he could too.

Taking the hint, Ryder knelt between my legs. He cupped my knee, inched his hand beneath my dress, and pushed the fabric up to my waist.

As much as I wanted him to kiss me, I couldn't help but stare into his dark eyes. They looked at me like I was the only thing that existed in his world. And maybe I did for the moment. The scruff on his jaw was dark, like he hadn't shaved in a couple days. His eyes told a story but before I could find out what that was, he lowered his mouth to mine.

I sighed, opening to him and taking his tongue deep between my lips.

The kiss became frantic.

His hands roamed and massaged, kneading into my skin until I was a panting, aching mess. "Tell me to stop," he murmured against my lips.

"No." I reached between us, unbuckling his belt and lowering the zipper to his fly.

He pulled my hands away, shoving them above my head. Holding my wrists in one hand, he stared down at me and winked.

My stomach fluttered. That damn wink was enough to make me lose all control.

He reached back between us, brushing his knuckles over my center.

I chewed my bottom lip, my thighs shaking at the soft contact.

He smirked, sitting back.

My gaze dropped to his waist. Holy hell. His length was long and thick. It had been so long for me; I was sure he was going to rip me in half.

Ryder reached into his pocket and pulled out a condom.

My heart sped up, watching him open the package.

"You want to help me?" he asked, a teasing lilt to his voice.

I pulled the rubber from the package and slipped it down the length of him.

A low groan rumbled from his chest, his eyes fluttering closed.

I kissed his chin, a breathless laugh escaping me. "You like that?"

"You have no idea." He pushed me onto my back, cupping my thigh and spreading me wide for him.

"Ryder." I ran a thumb over his bottom lip.

He reached between us and hooked his finger in the crotch of my panties. Pulling it to the side, he took a deep breath.

"Wait." I looked down between us, but I couldn't see anything. The fabric of his shirt was in the way. "I want to wat—" He sank into me in a rough thrust. I cried out, my thighs shaking around him.

"Fuck." His lips found the side of my throat, his hips powering forward and back in smooth, unforgiving thrusts.

I was experienced but nothing compared to this moment with him. The pleasure was almost too much. It forced tears to my eyes at how good Ryder felt inside of me. "Ple...Go..." My words came out broken, a jumbled mess much like my heart.

Ryder inched his hand up my hip. His body shook, his back muscles twitching over his bones.

"Faster," I heard myself say.

He grunted, his teeth sinking into the soft spot beneath my ear. His hips picked up speed, powering into me with so much strength, my back bowed off the bed of the truck.

Ryder leaned his forehead against mine, linking our fingers.

Staring up at him, I licked my lips.

He smirked, took the hint, and lowered his mouth to mine.

FIVE

RYDER

SHE WAS PERFECT. ALMOST too perfect.

Her body was hot, wet, and all mine for the night.

I never had any intentions of fucking her tonight but when she looked at me with those beautiful blue eyes of hers and ran her thumb along my mouth, I couldn't resist. I had to feel her lips against mine. If she had turned me away, just knowing what she felt like against me, would have been enough.

Even though I was shipping out on Monday, I made it a personal mission to keep in contact with her. Other people did it. So we could as well. Couldn't we?

"Ryder." Clara's moan pulled me from my thoughts. "Please."

I lifted off of her and leaned back. Glancing down at our joined bodies, I ran my thumb along her swollen clit.

She jumped, her breath catching.

Before I could stop myself, I pulled from her body and flipped her onto her stomach. Landing a hard swat against the seat of her ass, I shivered at the way she arched into my swing.

Towering back over her, I covered her hands and slowly slid back into her body.

She whimpered, her pussy sucking me in even deeper.

"You're mine tonight, aren't you?" I whispered, licking along the shell of her ear.

"Yes," she panted.

"You like my fat cock deep inside your cunt, baby?" I kissed the corner of her mouth. "Tell me," I demanded when she didn't answer.

"Yes." She trembled beneath me. "Yes, I love it."

I chuckled. "You're giving me some going away present. I'll be thinking of this the whole time I'm away."

"If you jerk off to thoughts of this moment, I want a video."

A laugh boomed through me. "It's a fucking deal."

Wrapping myself around her, I slammed my pelvis against the seat of her ass. As much as I wanted to turn her back over and kiss her, I needed this moment. This sense of control that she was giving me. Because I knew that once I ended up in that shithole and was doing my job, I would have no control at all. The only thing I had to strive for was supporting my country and making it a better place for this generation and the next and so on. My ancestors did it. My father did it. It was my turn and there was no going back now.

"Ryder?"

I jumped, finding Clara looking up at me over her shoulder.

"You good?" she asked, her brows furrowing in the middle.

Covering her, I nipped the base of her neck, not needing her to see that I was terrified to leave. "I am now," I said, because there was no way I would tell her different.

SIX

Clara

I REALIZED RATHER QUICKLY that there was a different side to Ryder. He was sweet, kind, and gentle, but get him in bed and it was a whole different story. It had been a few hours since he used my body good and hard like we both wanted. Now he was softly snoring beside me with his arm wrapped around my middle.

He hugged me tighter against him, pushing his face into the crook of my neck and letting out a soft sigh.

A light laugh escaped me.

"Something funny?" he asked, his voice gruff.

"No. Just happy."

He threw a leg over mine and nipped the spot beneath my ear. "Good."

We laid like that for as long as we could. But I knew that he had things to do before leaving on Monday. I wished I could have asked him to spend the day with me, but it wouldn't have been fair of me to do that. Knowing he had to spend time with his family, I kept my mouth shut. His mom and sisters were probably freaking out already. I imagined his dad being broody and grumpier than usual. I had only met Angel a handful of times and even though he was a little moody, you could see the pride he had for his son.

"I hope you have fun with your family tonight," I told Ryder when he put the truck into park in the parking lot of my apartment building.

"Thank you." He turned toward me and grabbed my hand. "Thank you for last night."

"And this morning?" I winked.

He chuckled, kissing my knuckles.

After we had packed up and Ryder put the cover back on the bed of the truck, he had shoved me against the side of it. I could still feel his face between my legs and the burn of his scruff on my inner thighs.

"I couldn't help myself." He shrugged.

"I wasn't complaining."

His eyes twinkled. "Good." He hesitated. "Did you want me to walk you up?"

"You know you won't be leaving soon if you do that, right?"

Ryder released my hand and left the truck. When he came around to my side, he opened the passenger door. "Tell me no."

I laughed, jumping out of the vehicle. "Come. I have coffee and I can cook you breakfast, and I can even introduce you to every corner of my bed. Not exactly in that order." I backed up, waggling my eyebrows.

A wicked grin spread on his face, when he charged for me.

I squealed, running to the apartment building.

By the time we were on my floor, I was panting and he looked like he hadn't just run up three flights of stairs. I clearly needed to work out more.

"Hurry up, baby. I'm not a patient man."

28

PROMISE US

I ran down the hall to my apartment. As soon as I had the door unlocked, a hard body pressed up against me. I half expected Ryder to take it fast but instead, he spent the next hour savoring every inch of me.

While I was standing in front of the stove, cooking him eggs, a sense of peace washed over me. I was wearing his dress shirt and he was in his dress pants only. I realized rather quickly that I could fall for him. With his sexy smirk, his sweet advances, and dirty words, I was already waiting for him to come home from his deployment.

"I'll miss you." He stepped up behind me, placing a soft peck on my neck. "I do need to leave after breakfast though."

My chest tightened. "I know."

"You have my number. Text me. Call me. Send me videos. What the fuck ever." He turned me around, cupping my face. "I want more of this. I want to continue this. If you do as well that is."

My heart jumped. "Yes." I threw my arms around his neck. "I do. God do I ever."

He chuckled, placing a hard peck on my mouth. "Good."

After we ate, I walked Ryder to my door. I never realized that I would actually be sad to see him go. I thought last night would just be a one-time thing, we would move on and nothing else would come of this.

But as he stared down at me with those dark eyes of his, I fell. And I fell hard.

SEVEN

RYDER

A while later...

MY VISION FADED IN and out. A sharp pain stabbed me in the side, reminding me that I was still very much alive. I wasn't sure how or why. They should have just killed me already. I didn't know what they wanted. I couldn't even understand half the shit they were saying. But I was an American soldier. I had all the answers. I would have rolled my eyes if I could keep them open.

But they had no idea. They could try and get whatever they wanted from me, but I was trained. Even my father didn't know half the shit I had done, and he was a Navy SEAL. He had done things. Seen things. Survived things to get back to my mother. I needed to do the same to get back to my family.

Clara.

Fucking hell, she probably thought I was dead. I hadn't texted her back in God knew how long. But I couldn't. It wasn't safe. Our camp had been ambushed. Men and women died. My brothers were beaten and tortured, while my sisters...I swallowed past the bile burning my throat. I would never get the images of what was done to them out of my head. They weren't blood. None of them were blood but it went far past that. I reacted the same way as if they were my own flesh. I kept thinking of Gigi and Meadow and what I would have done if it were them who were beaten, raped, and mutilated.

A heavy fist landed against my cheek, the bone beneath the skin shattering. I was now numb to the pain. They could hit me. Beat me. Fucking kill me. Nothing they did would get what they wanted from me. No matter how hard they tried, my lips were sealed and the secrets I knew were safe.

But I knew...hell, I had known even before I was taken...there was no way I could come back from this or that things would ever be normal again.

I just prayed with everything in me that Clara would be patient with me. I liked her a lot and knew that what we had could turn into something more.

Wait for me, Clara, and I promise, baby, it'll be worth it.

But even I knew that some promises were meant to be broken.

PART TWO

ONE

Clara

RYDER IS HOME.

Those three words stared at me from the small screen on my cell phone. They had been words I longed to see for awhile now but a part of me never thought I would.

The text came in about a half hour ago from Gigi, Ryder's oldest sister. She had promised to keep me informed as soon as she heard anything about her brother. But to read that he was actually home, finally after all of this time, forced nerves to settle deep within my belly.

After our date, that felt well over a lifetime ago, we had kept in contact. Even after Ryder was deployed, we stayed in touch.

But about two months into his deployment, he just stopped responding. I knew that things had been good between us. We hadn't fought or anything like that. It wasn't like we hung out enough to fight anyway. He took me on a date and we slept together several times. It was my little going away present for him. I wasn't always one to sleep with a guy the night of the first date but sometimes it happened and I wasn't ashamed to admit it. A girl needed a little fun every now and again.

Ryder had left my place early the following afternoon to attend a going away party that his family had thrown for him and I hadn't seen him seen since.

I knew his family would have kept me informed if something had happened to him. Even though I had known that though, a part of me still feared that he would be killed while on deployment. I also knew his family and friends also feared the same.

When several weeks had passed where I didn't get a response to my texts, I tried reaching out to him again, but he never responded.

I had something I needed to tell him.

Not that I wanted to do it over the phone but I needed him to know before he came home.

His parents hadn't told him my little secret and I knew that once he found out, he would probably be pissed that he didn't know. But it wasn't for lack of trying on our part.

Gigi told me the had been home for about a week but had to go through some shit, her words, now that he was discharged from the Navy. She also reassured me that he would contact me as soon as he was able. It made me wonder if she wasn't just saying that to make me feel better and maybe Ryder didn't actually want to contact me. These thoughts weren't rational but I had never felt this away about a guy before. I was confused and just wanted to see Ryder to tell him my secret and get it done and over with so we could all move on.

Now that he was home and I would eventually see him again, I was nervous. I imagined him being so overjoyed to see me that he would wrap me up in a big hug and spin me around.

But if something had happened to him during his deployment and that was why he was discharged, he could also be different.

The buzzing suddenly coming from my phone, made me jump. This time, it was from Meadow. Ryder's other sister.

Ryder is home but he's changed.

My stomach twisted at those words.

It was one thing I appreciated about her. She was honest and didn't beat around the bush.

I loved them both like sisters I never had. Ryder's family treated me well and took me under their wing since I didn't see my brother often. He had interned for a friend's husband but after gaining some experience, he made a life-altering decision and moved to Europe. We talked often but not nearly as much as we used to.

I was going to text Meadow back and ask her just how much Ryder had changed but that conversation would be a little too much over texting. So instead, I just responded and said that I was looking forward to seeing him. Which I was. But if he changed like she said he did, it made me wonder if maybe he wasn't interested in me anymore.

Setting my phone on silent, I plugged it in and went to the kitchen to grab a glass of water.

Once I had my water, I headed back to my room and saw the screen on my cell flashing. Rushing to it, I noticed an unknown number calling me.

Under normal circumstances, I wouldn't have answered the phone, especially when it said unknown number. But ever since Ryder had been deployed, I answered the phone at every ring, no matter who was calling. Most were telemarketers. Some were his parents, his sisters' friends. But it had never been the person that I wanted to speak to most.

What Ryder and I had, was new and fresh.

Fun.

While we didn't know each other well, I still felt like he had a part of me I had never given to someone else. My brother told me that I was in love with Ryder. I laughed it off because there was no way that I could fall in love with someone so quickly.

Could I?

I had heard about it happening. I wasn't stupid. Love at first sight and all. But it had never been my thing. Especially when the guys I had been attracted to were few and far between anymore. Or they wanted one thing and that was it. But now that I was older, and Ryder and I had started seeing each other, I just wanted him. I wanted a relationship. Someone I could go home to and wake up next to in the morning. While what we had physically had been short-lived, it was the best thing I had ever experienced in my life. But if he changed like Meadow said, I wondered if he changed in the bedroom as well. Not that it mattered. It was his personality I liked most. The rest was just an added bonus.

Answering my phone, I let out a breathy, "Hello". There was a pause on the other end.

When no answer came, I thought maybe I hadn't answered in time and the person had hung up. But when a deep "Hi" sounded in my ear, I collapsed to the floor.

TWO

RYDER

As soon as Clara answered the phone, I was brought back to our one and only date. It had felt like years ago since I wined and dined her, literally, in the back of my pickup truck. It had been an idea from my sisters. I had a mattress spread out in the bed of my truck, along with Christmas twinkle lights surrounding it. We ate and drank some wine, laughed, talked, and got to know one another. I had asked her out on a whim and the next day, we promised each other that we would see where this went.

But after I was deployed, while we did keep in contact, it didn't last long. That was on me. Especially when my assignment had gone to shit, and I couldn't make contact with anyone for months. Being an explosives technician, I had a dangerous job. But I never thought it would have gone down how it did. I was sure most thought I, along with a few members of my team, were dead. Thankfully we made it out safe and sound. We had some emotional scars that we had to work through. They happened when we were beat and tortured to give information. I didn't cave. But I couldn't say the same for some of my team.

"Ryder?"

Clara's breathy voice brought me back to the present.

"Hi."

"Hi." She laughed lightly. "Your sisters texted me and told me you were home. I wanted to contact you, but I wasn't sure how to reach you. And I didn't want to take you away from your family."

"I appreciate that." *I want to see you.* That thought forced nerves to settle deep in my gut. Nerves that had never been there. But it had been so long, I wasn't sure where she stood.

"Can I see you?" she asked softly.

"Yes," I answered a little too abruptly.

Clara giggled. "I missed you too."

I chuckled, running a hand through my hair. "I *did* miss you. More than I could ever tell you."

My parents had asked me if I had seen Clara. Which I thought was odd. Especially when they didn't know her. Clara did work at The Dove Project, but other than that, I wasn't sure why Clara would be asked about.

"You can come over tomorrow evening. I still live at the same place."

"I'd love that. A lot actually," I confessed.

"Me too."

A smile spread on my face. "Good." I paused, unsure if I should tell her to have a good night and that I would see her tomorrow or if we should spend some time catching up. Even if it was just over the phone.

Suddenly, a soft noise sounded in the background.

"I'll be back," Clara said quickly.

I frowned, wondering why she wouldn't just take her cell with her.

A few minutes later, Clara returned, the phone shuffling as she moved around. "Sorry about that."

"Everything good?" I asked, moving to my bed. I glanced around my childhood bedroom, appreciating that my parents left it the same as it was before I'd been deployed.

"Yes, it is now. So..." She paused. "How are you doing?"

That was the question, wasn't it? How *was* I doing?

"My therapist says I'm making progress." I shrugged even though she couldn't see me. "So, I guess that's a start."

"Meadow said you'd changed." Clara cleared her throat. "You sound the same to me though."

"Maybe I have changed. I don't know. A lot of shit went down in the last few months. Shit I prefer not to think about. My therapist makes me do enough of that."

"Well, I hope he's helping you."

"She is." I waited.

"Oh."

I chuckled, shaking my head. "Jealous, baby?"

Clara snorted. "As fucking if."

"Alright." I leaned back against the headboard. "If you say so."

"I am not jealous. I have no reason to be when we..." She coughed. "Well, you know."

"No, Clara. I don't actually know. So, tell me." I sat forward, needing to hear her words. Needing to hear that I wasn't crazy and that we could make this work. Even though it had been quite a while since I had seen her, we had a connection from the moment we met. We had made plans to continue dating, seeing each other, whatever the fuck you wanted to call it, even while I had been deployed. It would have worked too, especially when we texted, and talked on the phone, and video chatted as much as possible but then a few of my squad, as well as myself, were taken hostage and the rest was fucking history.

"I don't know, Ryder." Clara had a bite in her tone that made my dick twitch. "I haven't seen you in forever. I haven't talked to you until now. A part of me thought you were dead. I just..."

"I know." I sighed. "I'm fine. A little fucked up as a result but I'm good."

41

"Are you sure?" she asked gently. "I mean, if you aren't, I understand. I don't want you thinking you have to be strong or anything just for me or for...well...I just want you happy."

I smiled, my heart jumping at her words. "I appreciate that, Clara. But I promise that I'm good."

"I missed you."

"I missed you too." And I did. Fuck me did I ever.

"I know we didn't have a lot of time to get to know each other but with our video calls and texts, I'd like to think it helped a bit."

"It did. You know me more than any other woman I've ever dated."

"Really?" I could hear the smile in her voice. "I do?"

"Yeah, baby. You do."

We spent the next little bit talking about anything and everything. I learned that she had finally gotten her degree to become a social worker. She had told me way back when that she wanted to help children find their happy and safe homes. It had warmed my heart then and warmed my heart even more now.

It was pushing midnight when I heard her yawn. We said our goodbyes and promised to meet up the next evening for dinner. Neither of us referred to it as a date and I wondered why. It wasn't like I had been interested in anyone else. Clara Blanco had fascinated me from the beginning, and I couldn't wait to explore this more with her now that I was home.

For good.

THREE

Clara

TO SAY I WAS nervous was an understatement.

Besides the fact that I hadn't seen Ryder in well over a year, I had something to tell him. A big something. I tried telling him months ago but when he disappeared and none of us could get a hold of him, I had to keep this big thing from him. I was sure he would be pissed when he found out, but I couldn't dwell on that.

When I stared down at the very reason I existed anymore, I couldn't help but smile.

My son, Ryder's son, James, cooed and babbled, slapping his chubby hands against my cheeks. I laughed, tickling his belly. "I'm going on a date with your daddy tonight."

James continued talking in his own little way. Maybe he was encouraging me and telling me that it would be alright.

Although Ryder and I hadn't seen each other in quite a while, I still felt like I knew him. For the most part anyway. I knew that he would accept James. I didn't expect him to jump into a relationship with me. I just wanted him there for our son. That was all that mattered to me.

The one and only date we had been on, resulted in me getting pregnant. I remembered back to when I found out. I was scared and nervous to tell him but after talking to his sisters, I became excited. We went to call Ryder together, but he never answered. I spent my pregnancy keeping it from Ryder. Not by my choice, of course, but it still felt like I was betraying him in a way.

Now I was even more terrified to tell him.

Should I invite him over and let him meet James and then tell him that he was the father? Or should I just come out and say that I had his baby? I wasn't sure how to break the news to him gently.

Once the time to meet Ryder at a local restaurant came around, I decided that I would tell him over dinner. He was supposed to come over to my place, but we ended up deciding that we would go out instead. I didn't want to keep this from him anymore, so I had to tell him tonight. His family had been nothing but supportive when I told them that I wanted to tell Ryder myself.

As soon as I was about to leave my apartment to bring James to Ryder's parents' place, my phone dinged.

When I checked the incoming text, my heart sunk.

Ryder: I'm sorry but I can't meet up for dinner tonight.

He was cancelling through text? He didn't have the decency to actually call me?

Instead of responding, I called him up. Part of me expected it to go to voicemail, so when his deep voice greeted me, I hesitated before saying anything.

"You're cancelling our dinner plans? Why?" I asked him instead of greeting him back.

"Something's come up. I have to help my dad with...something."

My chest tightened. He was lying.

"Okay, well I had something to tell you, but I guess it's going to have to wait. Take care, Ryder."

"What did you have to tell me?"

I disconnected the call instead of answering. I was getting too old for this shit.

Glancing in the mirror I had hung on the wall in the hallway, I let out a harsh sigh. I had spent over an hour getting ready for dinner. It had been a long time since I had dressed up to go anywhere. I was finally baby puke free and now I was stuck at home.

A thought came to me.

No. Fuck Ryder.

I was still going to go out for dinner.

After I finished getting James ready, I headed over to Ryder's parents' place. I knew Ryder's mom, Jay, would ask questions. His dad, not so much.

When I entered their home, I was hit by a delicious scent that smelled like homemade bread. Jay had taught herself to bake over the past few months. She had told me once that it was relaxing and helped take her mind off of her missing son.

"We're in the kitchen, Clara," Jay called out.

Placing the car seat on the ground, I pulled James from it and hugged him to my chest. "Let's go see Grandma and Grandpa," I told him.

He sighed, snuggling his face into the crook of my neck. My heart warmed every time he did that. I never knew how much I could love another human being until I had him.

When I entered the kitchen, I saw Angel, Ryder's dad, sitting at the table and Jay hovering by the counter, flipping through what looked like a recipe book.

"Hey, sweetheart." Jay came towards me. "How are you and how's my grandbaby?"

"He's good and I'm...well...you know." I only shrugged. I didn't want to talk ill of Ryder knowing that he was their son but the fact that he cancelled our plans, hurt.

"What's wrong?" Angel asked, his eyes snapping to mine. "Who am I killing?"

"Um...well I'm not sure you'd be down for offing your son." I tried laughing it off but instead, my throat burned, and my eyes welled.

"Sit." Jay took James from me, bouncing him gently in her arms. "And spill."

I did as I was told and told them about the dinner plans that Ryder cancelled. "He said that he has to help you with something," I told Angel.

Angel frowned, looking between his wife and me. "I don't know what he's talking about. I'm staying in with Jay and we're watching movies and pigging out on popcorn. And watching James of course."

I knew this was the case, but it still hurt to hear it. Obviously, Ryder didn't want to see me.

"I don't think that's what it is," Jay said gently.

My cheeks burned, not realizing I had spoken out loud. "I want to tell him about James but now that he's home, I don't want to do it over the phone. I know either way, he's going to be pissed. I hope he doesn't think I kept this from him on purpose because I didn't."

"I know, darling." Angel ran a hand through his graying hair. "We would never think that of you. We tried to tell him but..." A dark shadow passed over his aging face. "Well...you know."

Jay sat beside Angel, holding James close to her chest. "We love you and we love you for Ryder but whatever happens, I do know my son. He will be there for James. No matter what."

A part of me wanted him to be there for me too.

A selfish and lonely part.

"I know. I do know that." I sighed. "That's all that matters."

Ryder's parents only stared at me. They meant well but their words of encouragement didn't help me at the moment.

I quickly said my goodbyes, kissed my son on the head and left the house.

If Ryder didn't want to date me, then I would date myself. I hadn't been out for dinner in quite a while, especially not alone. I would take advantage of this quiet time and try not to think of the man who invaded my every waking thought.

FOUR

RYDER

I WAS A PUSSY.

It was a straight up fact that I was terrified. I never knew how terrified I was until the dinner plans with Clara snuck up on me. I wasn't sure if it was my PTSD or something completely different, but I cancelled the plans before I could think twice about it.

When she called me to demand to know why I cancelled, I could hear the hurt in her voice. We had never said that it was a date. We just wanted to meet up and see each other. So why the hell did I fucking cancel?

That was two nights ago, and I couldn't get Clara out of my head. I should have gone to her first. Right when I got home, I should have rushed to her. Even if she changed her mind and didn't actually want to pursue this further, at least I would have tried. I respected the hell out of her and I never expected her to wait for me. Even though she made that promise and I did the same, things happen. Time happened.

I had stopped by The Dove Project to see my mom and to also find out if she needed help with anything. But I was not expecting the third degree from her.

"Why did you cancel your dinner plans with Clara?" Mom asked as soon as I stepped foot into her office.

I hesitated at the door, keeping one hand on the doorknob in case I needed to bolt. "What are you talking about?"

"You had dinner plans with Clara and cancelled. I'm asking you why."

Since when did my mother care about the plans I made with women? Especially when I cancelled them. She never once questioned me on it.

"I didn't know you knew about that." It probably sounded dumb, but I really had no idea what else to say.

"I know everything." Mom tapped her temple. "I'm a mom. We see and know all."

Somehow, I didn't doubt that.

"So, tell me what happened. You said you had to help your dad with something which isn't true. Why would you lie?"

"Did Clara talk to you?" I knew they had become closer since Clara volunteered at the center from time to time, but I didn't know they were close to the point Clara felt comfortable enough to complain about me. She and I needed to have a little chat.

Mom scowled. "Just answer the question, Ryder."

I sighed, scrubbing a hand down my face. "I'm scared, alright? I like her. I like her a lot. But I haven't seen her in over a year and I'm scared that she no longer wants to date me or she found someone else or..." I knew I had...issues. While it wasn't as serious as some, it still kept me up at night. I had heard horror stories of people with PTSD waking up with their hands around their partners' throats or worse.

"Ryder." Mom closed the distance between us and placed her hands on my shoulders. "You need to see her. Even if you two just stay as friends, you really need to see her."

I frowned. "Okay but—"

"No." Mom cupped my cheek. "Just trust me on this."

"I'll talk to her." I figured there was no point in arguing with her. My sister Meadow had been the only one who could truly get away with that. It paid to be the youngest kid sometimes.

"Good. Now go so I can actually get some work done."

I chuckled. "Love you, Mama."

"I love you too." Her eyes shone. "And I'm so glad you're home safely." And for good went unsaid. She never said it, but I knew that she was happy that I was discharged from the Navy. Even though she was proud of me, I could see the lines of worry written all over her face. Now that I was home, she was worried for different reasons. It came with the cost of being a parent.

Leaving Mom's office, I headed out to the main area of the center. Giving the receptionist a nod and a little wave, I went to leave when I heard my sister's voice coming from the hall. Meadow may have been tiny, but her voice carried, especially when she was excited about something.

"Did you see these new pictures of James? Clara put him in a construction onesie and he's so freaking cute. He's getting so big too. I can't believe how much he looks like—"

Before I knew what I was doing, I was back in the hall and stomping toward my sister. She was talking to a few of the other girls who worked at the center.

It was like I was having an out of body experience. I saw myself grabbing Meadow's phone. There was no reason for it really, but I couldn't stop myself.

"Hey! What the hell, Ryder," Meadow demanded, attempting to reach for her phone.

Turning away from her, I looked down at the small screen. It was a group chat between Meadow, Clara and a few other people I could only assume were Clara's friends or family. I wasn't sure. But what caught my attention was the fact that there was an image of a baby. He looked to be about only a few months old.

"Who is this?" I heard myself ask.

"He's my son."

FIVE

Clara

I DIDN'T WANT RYDER to find out like this but when he looked my way, I realized that he didn't know exactly who James was.

Ryder didn't say anything as he stared at me.

Meadow grabbed her phone from him but I imagined it was only because he let her.

It was unnerving how he looked at me and didn't utter a single word. I had to admit, he looked good. But it wasn't the time to think of how hot the guy was when we had other things to talk about. And fast. Especially before he completely lost it.

Much to my surprise, he turned on his heel and stomped out of the center.

"He doesn't know," Meadow said, her hand fluttering to her throat.

"I haven't seen him to tell him." I walked past her to go search for Ryder and deal with this mess. "I'll talk to him." I rushed out of the building, looking around the parking lot. Ryder was pacing back and forth by a vehicle, his hands shoved in his pockets. It was starting to rain. It was a welcomed distraction, but it wasn't enough.

"Ryder." I went up to him but kept my distance. He was unhinged and I didn't really want to get too close where it spooked him, and he rushed off. We *had* to talk.

"How could you?"

My eyes widened at his question. His voice was laced with pain.

"We promised each other that we would try and make things work. Even though it would be long distance, you promised me." He shook his head. "I'm a damn fool."

"No, you aren't." The rain was starting to come down harder, soaking us beneath our clothes. "Come with me to my place. We need to talk about this."

He scoffed, rolling his eyes. "Right, Clara. I remember how things were when we got back to your apartment. Or do you have a house now? What else has changed? Am I going to go into your home only to be met by your husband?"

"What? No. Not at all." I closed that final space between us. "Please, come home with me. I can explain everything."

"Explain what?" he yelled. "I know we weren't in a serious relationship, but I never expected you to get pregnant by some other fucker."

"Excuse me, but that never happened." I placed my hands on my hips, glaring up at him. "I tried telling you. All of us did. But then you disappeared. We thought you were dead. We didn't want to think it, of course, but no one would tell us anything. Then you come home, and I tried meeting up with you but you cancelled our plans remember?"

"Hold the fuck on. You said he's your son. If you didn't get pregnant by someone else..." Ryder's voice trailed off, his eyes widening.

Crossing my arms under my chest, I lifted my chin. "Figure it out, Ryder?" I didn't want him to find out this way, but I also didn't appreciate what he accused me of either.

"He's...I have...fuck." Ryder ran a hand through his hair. "Really?"

I took a step in the direction of my car. "I think we need to talk."

"Clara."

I turned, facing Ryder as he came toward me. His head hung; his hands were back in his pockets. He looked like a puppy who got caught peeing on the floor.

"I didn't know," he murmured.

"I know." I went up to him, placing my hand on his chest. "I made a promise to you, and it was a promise that I've kept and still intend to keep. As long as you'll let me. I didn't get pregnant by another guy. *You* got me pregnant, Ryder. That first night together. The next morning. I don't know when. But it was one of those many times we shared that got me pregnant." Moving my hand up to his shoulder, I let it roam down the length of his arm.

He shivered under my touch.

"You have a son, Ryder."

His breath caught. "James."

"I named him after my grandfather," I said gently, linking my fingers in his. "James is at your parents' place. Your dad is watching him. We can pick him up and then head to my place and talk." *Please say yes.*

"I'd like that."

Ryder let me lead him to my car.

The whole drive to his parents' place, I was on edge. His reaction to having a son went better than I thought it would.

"I've been told several times that I shouldn't pine over you or that I should move on, but I never had time and I like to think that there's something special between us. But I don't expect us to have a relationship, Ryder. I would like you in James' life as much as possible though."

Ryder placed a hand on my thigh. "I'll be there. Every step of the way for him." He gave me a squeeze. "And for you too."

A breath I didn't realize I had been holding, left me. Add to the fact that he was touching me. After all of this time. After thinking at one point that I would never see him again. He was touching me.

Now that he knew about his son, I was even more nervous. I made him a promise and had waited for him this whole time. Not that I had a whole lot of free time to date anyway. But since he was home and for good, I wasn't sure how this would turn out.

Making a promise with myself, I would go into this with an open mind and see where the night took us.

SIX

RYDER

I HAD A SON.

It made sense now.

I had been asked several times since I returned home, if I had seen Clara or not. Everyone knew that we had gone on a date before I was deployed more than a year ago, but I assumed most would think it was just something fun. Like a way to blow off some steam before I was thrown into hell. Literally.

When we arrived at my parents' place, I was out of the car before Clara put it into park. I was vaguely aware of her calling out my name, but I couldn't focus. All I could see in my mind's eye was my son. A baby boy I only just found out I had a hand in creating.

Once I reached the front porch to my parents' place, I went to open the door when Clara caught my hand.

"I need to see him," I heard myself tell her.

"I know but I just want you to know that your parents knew." She shook her head. "I mean, of course they knew. You obviously know that. But what I'm saying is that they promised me they wouldn't tell you until I could. So please don't be mad at them. If anything, be mad at me instead."

"I'm not mad." I cupped her cheek. "Shocked yes. I thought we just had some fun. I didn't realize we created a new life together."

Her eyes shone. "He's perfect."

"So are you." I wasn't expecting to say those words since we were just reunited, but with the smile pulling at her lips, I was glad I did.

"Let's introduce you to your son, Ryder." Something else flashed in her eyes. Something foreign. Something I definitely wanted to explore later.

Entering the house I had grown up in, I was greeted by my dad. His eyes widened when they landed on us. He looked down at the small baby boy in his arms, back to me, back to the baby.

"He's mine," I whispered.

Dad smiled, nodding. "He is."

"He finally knows," Clara said from behind me.

I closed the distance between my father and I and stared down at James. He had a head of dark hair, long black lashes, and a tanned complexion that mirrored my own.

"Can I hold him?" I asked no one in particular.

"He's your son, Ryder." Clara came up to our sides. "Of course, you can hold him."

"Hold your boy." Dad handed him to me, his voice thick.

When James was placed in my arms, everything fell into place.

All my worries.

All my fears.

Everything I had worked so damn hard for, the stress, anxiety, every single fucking thing, disappeared as I stared down into my son's eyes.

SEVEN

Clara

I KNEW THIS DAY would come. It had been something I longed for ever since I found out I was pregnant. But actually seeing Ryder hold his son, finally, after all of this time, I couldn't help the tears rolling down my cheeks.

Ryder's head lifted, his back stiffening. He looked my way. Something flashed behind his eyes. Something I had never seen before. Not in him. Hell, not in anyone I had been interested in. I couldn't place what it was exactly, but it sent a shiver down my spine nonetheless.

"I'll give you some privacy." Angel clapped Ryder's shoulder before heading down the hall that led to his office.

"Come here." Ryder's demand made my cheeks heat. I was sure they were red, but he never said anything. Meadow said he had changed but I wasn't sure by how much.

Wiping my cheeks, I closed the distance between us.

Much to my surprise, Ryder leaned down to my ear and took a deep inhale. When he let out his breath, a low purr followed.

"Tell me about those tears," he murmured against my skin.

I had been worried that maybe the attraction was no longer there but holy hell, was I ever wrong.

"I'm happy," I confessed, staring up at the man who had given me the greatest gift I had ever received. "I was worried how you would react to getting me pregnant. It wasn't like we dated for long."

"That night with you, followed by the next morning, had been the greatest hours of my damn life, Clara." Ryder kissed my cheek before heading to the couch. He sat, holding James tight in his arms. "I should have gone to you right when I got home. I'm sorry I didn't. I was scared."

My eyes widened. "Really? You were scared? Why?"

"I thought maybe you'd found someone else. I wouldn't have blamed you though."

"I made you a promise, Ryder. But it wasn't like I had time to date or anything."

"I'm glad you didn't date," Ryder said, which came out more as a growl.

I laughed, my cheeks heating. Running my hand through my hair, I pulled the long ends over my shoulder. Being here with him, sent a flutter through my belly.

"How did everything go? With the pregnancy and delivery and everything?"

I joined him on the couch, running a hand over James's head. "It was the hardest thing I've ever done. I'm not going to lie and sugarcoat it. It sucked. Not all of it, of course. By the time I reached eight months, I was definitely ready for it to be over. But when he was placed in my arms, none of that mattered."

"I'm sorry I wasn't here."

"Don't." I placed my hand on Ryder's arm. "I'm not telling you this to make you feel guilty. You asked, so I'm being honest."

"Do you have pictures or anything?"

"I do. Your sisters helped me, and I ended up ordering photo books online that show my pregnancy progress. I also have so many pictures of James, it's unreal." I laughed. "I'm sure he'll get sick of them when he gets older, so I'll do it while I can."

"I want to go home with you."

My head snapped up. "You do?"

Ryder scowled. "Fuck, I mean…I just…" He handed me James and stood from the couch. He began pacing, running his hands through his hair. "Listen, I know we're doing everything backwards, but I meant what I said during our one and only date. I wanted to explore this more with you then and I still do."

"I want that too," I whispered.

Ryder knelt in front of me. "You do?"

"I do. I'd say I want to take things slow, but I think we've moved past that."

He smirked. "Just a little bit."

Holding James in one arm, I cupped Ryder's cheek with my free hand. "I'm glad you're home."

"Me too, baby." He kissed my palm. "I'm not going anywhere either. I'm home, for good."

"You sure? I mean…" I chewed my bottom lip. I didn't know what I meant. "I just…I don't want you to feel pressured. I know you'll be a father to James. You'll be the best father. But I don't expect us to have a relationship or anything."

"Clara."

"No." I shook my head. "I don't want you to feel like you have to be with me just because we have a son."

"Hey, listen to me." Ryder stood and sat beside me on the couch. "We started…whatever this is before I got you pregnant. We texted back and forth, and video chatted for weeks."

"I didn't know I was pregnant, so please don't think I kept it from you."

"Stop this." Ryder cupped my cheek, turning my head to meet the soft impact of his mouth on mine. His thumb brushed along my jaw, his strong grip holding my head in place. "I would never think that of you."

We had communicated for a bit in the beginning but then all of a sudden, he had disappeared. It was like as soon as I found out I was pregnant, the universe took him from me.

"I never thought I'd see you again." I looked down at James sleeping in my arms. "But then James was born and you were all I saw. He doesn't even look like me."

Silence fell between us. It was comfortable and needed in a way. I had meant everything I said. In the beginning, I longed for him to know that he had gotten me pregnant.

"We can take this slow." Ryder wrapped his arm around the base of my back. "We can go on another date and just take this one day at a time."

As much as I liked the sound of that, we both knew that it wouldn't be the case. Especially when we had slept together the first date we ever went on.

"It's been a long time," I murmured, hoping he would understand what I meant by that.

"It's been a long time for me too," he confessed. "I haven't been with anyone else since our night together."

I looked at him then. "Neither have I. Not that I've had any time. But even if I never would have had James, I still would have waited for you."

He raised an eyebrow. "Yeah?"

"Yes." I laughed. "There's no way I was giving that up." I nodded, glancing down at his crotch.

Ryder chuckled, rising to his full height. "Well, I think you should take me back to your apartment, so we can get James ready for bed together. Then whatever else happens, happens."

"Really?" We had been joking around but I would love for him to spend the night with me. Sure, maybe some would say it was too soon but was it really? No, not for us. I didn't think it was too soon in the least.

"I meant what I said, Clara." He held out his hand. "Don't doubt me."

Placing my hand in his, I let him pull me to my feet. I looked down at our son who was currently sleeping in my arms. I appreciated Ryder's words but at the same time I didn't want to end up with a broken heart either. It didn't matter how good the sex had been. I wanted more. Not just a casual fuck.

"Hey." Ryder pinched my chin, tilting my head back to meet his heated stare. "I like you. I wouldn't have asked you out if I didn't. Could this turn into more? Besides having a son together? Yes, I think it could. But I won't lie and say that I don't have PTSD. It's mild compared to most. But it's there. And I still get nightmares and all that shit."

"Meadow said you changed," I told him. "I'm not sure how exactly but I think she's right. I can feel it. That doesn't make sense but I..."

"I'm still the same man who took you on that date, baby. I promise. Am I a little moodier now? Yes, I am. But that will never be geared toward you. Any shit we fight about, we'll talk it through. I promise you that. I won't keep anything from you. I'm too old for games."

A breath of relief left me. It was like a weight had been lifted from my shoulders at hearing his words.

"Thank you," I whispered.

"Are you fine with me joining you tonight at your place? I don't have to spend the night, but I would like to hang out with you a little longer."

I nodded quickly. "Yes, please. I missed you."

"I missed you too." Ryder leaned down to my ear, his hot breath fanning over the side of my face. "In more ways than one."

EIGHT

RYDER

THE SHIVER THAT RIPPLED through Clara, made my dick twitch. Fucking her tonight had been the last thing on my mind but I knew her. Even though we were only just reunited, I knew that Clara was a woman who went after what she wanted. She was down for a hard fuck. Didn't matter that we had done things backwards and wanted to try and take things slow. Fucking her, would be slow. Dating her could come later. That was the part that we both had to be patient on.

We had said bye to my dad. As much as I wanted to stay and visit with him, I needed to get reacquainted with Clara and also get to know my son. I still couldn't believe I fathered a child. It was hard to wrap my head around but at the same time, I was excited to be his dad. I would spend the rest of my days teaching him what my own father taught me. I would instill all of the life lessons I had learned along the way and make things as easy as possible for him. Life was hard but I would show him that it was manageable with the right support system.

I would also show Clara the same. I had meant what I said when I told her I wasn't going anywhere. Even if we just remained friends and nothing more, I would be there every step of the way. A thought came to me where she ended up with someone who wasn't me. It left a bitter taste in my mouth and it made my stomach clench. Just the mere idea of another man touching her, made me want to commit murder.

"What's wrong?"

My gaze slid Clara's way at her question. "What do you mean?"

"You're scowling and acting all growly." She raised an eyebrow. "You okay?"

"I'm thinking what it would be like if you ended up with someone else," I blurted before I could stop myself.

"Oh." She laughed, looking back out at the road in front of us. "Trust me, Ryder. There's no one else I'm interested in. Even if nothing comes of this, I'm fine with being single. I have more important things to focus on anyway."

I heard what she was saying but I knew deep down, she needed that physical connection with someone. Because I needed the same.

"Promise me something." I reached over the console between us and cupped her inner thigh. Her breath caught but she only nodded. "Promise me that even if we don't end up in a relationship that if you ever just need a hard fuck, you call me. No one else. Just me."

Clara pulled the car into the parking lot of her apartment building. Putting it into park, she took a deep breath and then another before killing the engine.

"You have to promise me the same then." She turned her full body toward me, the movement making my hand inch a little higher up her thigh. "I don't want to end up hearing about you fucking some random woman just because you couldn't get a hold of me. You know where I live. You've been to my apartment before. I also had your son. So, you and I?" She waved a finger between us. "Whether we date, remain only friends, whatever it is, we sleep with each other. No one else."

"You know we're going to end up more than just friends."

"But you said—"

"I know what I said." In a quick move, I cupped her between her legs.

Her cheeks reddened, her teeth biting her full bottom lip set my blood on fire.

"I promise to call only you if I need to feel a hot, wet pussy." Before she could say any more, I left the car.

I needed to get it together for fear of throwing her to the ground, ripping off her clothes, and fucking her within an inch of her life. It had never been like this. Not with the others. From the moment Clara and I slept together months ago, I was hooked. I fell, and I fell damn hard.

"James is a good sleeper, but I'll let you feed him and then we can put him to bed," Clara said, walking past me with James in a stroller.

I closed the distance between us and gently pushed her aside, so I could push him instead. It was the least I could do when I was never around for her pregnancy, the birth, and the first few months of his life.

We made our way up to Clara's apartment in silence but no matter how quiet we were, I could almost hear the beating of her heart and her thoughts. Her eyes spoke volumes every time they glanced my way. She wanted more. Maybe not a full-on relationship tonight but she definitely wanted something. And I would give it to her. Whatever she wanted and no matter how she wanted it. I would make sure that by the end of the night, she would be happy, satiated, and maybe even passed out from pure exhaustion.

Once we reached her apartment, my hands gripped the bar of the stroller tighter. I was hit with memories of the one and only time I had been there. From the moment we had entered her home after our one and only date, we fucked. Everywhere. No wonder she got pregnant.

"I'll get his bottle ready." Clara cleared her throat, unlocked her door, and pushed her way inside.

Following her, I closed the door behind me and clicked the lock into place. I made a mental note to add more locks. My girl needed to be protected. At all costs.

My girl.

A smirk tugged at my lips.

I really liked the sound of that.

NINE

Clara

I WAS NERVOUS. MORE than nervous in fact. I was scared. Not of Ryder of course but of the sexual tension between us. Maybe scared was the wrong word but I was definitely anxious.

We quickly fell into a routine when getting James ready for bed. He had a messy diaper, but Ryder hadn't seemed to mind. He had said that he changed diapers for his sisters' kids whenever he could. They told him it was in the job description of being an uncle. But he said that he liked doing it because it gave him alone time with the kids so he could bond with them more, since he was never home. Not until now anyway. That warmed my heart of course.

Now we were in the living room, attempting to watch something on TV but I didn't think either of us were truly paying attention.

"Clara." Ryder cupped my hand that was resting on the couch between us.

My heart picked up speed, my stomach twisting and turning over itself as the butterflies fluttered through it.

I had never been nervous around the opposite sex before but with Ryder, because I really liked him and I also gave birth to his son, I didn't want to mess things up. Especially when they truly hadn't even started yet.

Taking a deep breath and then another, I channeled all of the confidence I had for as long as I could remember. Although, I hadn't really needed to use it much since James had been born. He didn't care if I was confident or not. As long as he had a clean diaper and a fully belly, he was happy.

Before Ryder could say anything more, I jumped up from the couch. Pulling off my sweater, I tossed it on the cushion beside him. It left me in a tiny tank top that showcased my full breasts. I was a double D before having James but now, I was bigger. Not by much but I definitely noticed that they were fuller. Turning around, I couldn't help the smile tugging at my lips as Ryder noticed as well.

His nostrils flared, a light pink hitting his cheeks.

"I breastfed for the first six to eight James was born but then dried up rather quickly. I don't know why. I guess it happens. But he never seemed to notice. I do get him the best formula I can though." It was expensive but I would do without first instead of having him not get the nutrients he needed.

"I'll help. In any way I can." Ryder's voice came out deep. Never knew he was a boob man.

Taking a step between his legs, I lowered onto his lap.

He swallowed hard, his hands gripping my hips.

"I think they're a cup bigger," I told him, brushing my thumb along his bottom lip. "My nipples are also more sensitive."

His breath caught. "They are, are they?"

Lifting the tank top up and over my head, my breasts swayed at the movement.

"Fuck," he whispered, licking his full mouth.

"It's been a long time, Ryder." I inched a little closer, feeling his breath on my tongue. "I haven't been touched since you. I can still remember what you feel like too. Your rough, calloused hands. Your thick cock." I moaned for added effect. "So fucking delicious."

The next thing I knew, I was thrown on my back. A gasp escaped me at the sudden movement.

"You thought you could seduce me, Clara?" Ryder growled, lowering his mouth to my nipple. "You thought you could remind me of what we've done and how fucking hot it was between us?" He bit down, licking along the area after to soothe the sting. "You want something, fucking say it."

"No." He knew what I wanted but it had been a while. So, I didn't mind waiting a little longer for it. I wanted him unhinged. I wanted to feel him throughout every inch of me and ache for days.

I wanted to fucking hurt.

Ryder lifted his head. "No? So, you don't want me to fuck you?"

"I never said that." I shoved him back as hard as I could and rolled off the couch. Landing on the floor with an oomph, I didn't get away fast enough when a heavy body covered me.

Rough hands ripped at my leggings and panties, forcing them down my legs.

With some maneuvering, I had them off of one leg.

Ryder ran his fingers through my hair, holding my head in place as he leaned down to my ear. "Didn't think we'd end up here. Not this fast anyway."

"I sure as hell did." I laughed.

He chuckled, kneeling between my spread legs. "We should be in a bed."

"No. I don't care about that. I don't need gentle or hearts and flowers. I just need this. Just you and me."

The sound of a zipper lowering sent a flush of heat over my already hot skin.

"Tell me you want me," he whispered against the soft spot by my ear.

"No." But we both knew that I did.

Ryder ran the tip of his cock over my center. "Fuck, baby. I don't know how long I'm going to last. You're fucking soaked."

"I don't care about that." I tried arching under him, but he was too strong for me. "Please, Ryder." As soon as I begged, he thrust into me in a smooth move.

A harsh cry left me, spots dancing in my vision at the delicious invasion I hadn't felt since our date over a year ago.

"Fucking hell." His mouth ran down the back of my neck to my shoulder. His thrusts were slow, powerful, and deep. His teeth sunk into my skin, surely leaving a mark.

Ryder slapped a hand on the ground by my head, picking up speed with his hips.

Grabbing onto his wrist, I held on as he fucked me on the floor in my living room.

"Clara," he groaned. "Your juicy cunt is taking it all, isn't it? You missed this. My big dick filling this tight little pussy."

"Yes," I whispered, his vulgar words making the tiny hairs on my body tingle with delight.

Ryder lifted himself off of me, grabbed my hips, and pulled me back as he thrust forward. "Such a good girl, taking that cock like a fucking champ."

I whimpered, the size of him stretching me almost to the point of painful. But it never quite reached it. Any deeper though and I would feel him in my soul.

"That's it, baby girl. Take all of me." His fingers dug into my ass cheeks.

That familiar tingle started in my toes, sliding up the backs of my legs until it reached the very center of me. His name left my lips on a hard cry. I had to bite my lip to keep from screaming for fear that I would wake up James.

"That's it." Ryder pulled me to an upright position, holding me against him. He wrapped his hand around my throat, inching his other between my legs. When he started strumming my clit, his fingers tightened on my jugular.

His name left my lips a second time in a matter of minutes.

Pushing me forward, he released me and stood.

72

I followed suit, needing more. Needing all of him in every sense of the word.

TEN

RYDER

AFTER FUCKING CLARA IN the living room, on the floor no less, we were finally in her bed. With my mouth fused to hers, I thrust my hips back and forth. She had come several times already and I came once. But I couldn't get enough. I refused to get enough. We had lots of time to make up for and there was no way I was stopping now.

"God, Ryder." She shivered beneath me. "I don't think I can come again."

"Give me one more." I kissed her softly, sucking her bottom lip between my teeth before gently biting down.

She yelped, lifting her hips at the same time.

It seemed that someone liked a little pain with her pleasure.

A half hour later and I decided to finally leave her alone. For now, anyway. We took a shower and cleaned up, but it was now at the point where I wasn't overly sure what to do.

Clara was standing in front of her dresser, slipping into pajamas, while I was sitting on the end of her bed. I couldn't help but watch her. She had gained some weight since having James and her blonde hair was darker and shorter than I remembered. Her skin was flawless, and her blue eyes lit up every time they landed on me. It sounded cliché but her eyes did have a twinkle in them. They shone? I didn't even fucking know but what I did know was that I enjoyed having them on me.

"I can feel you staring." She turned around once she was dressed and leaned against her dresser.

"Just memorizing you. Not because I'm leaving again but because I missed you. I don't want this to be a casual fuck." As I said the words, she came toward me. "I want more with you. I want to raise James together and I want…" I stared up at her as she stepped between my legs. "I want to fall in love with you."

A wide smile formed on Clara's face. "I want that too, baby. I want it all."

"Yeah?" I pulled her onto my lap, wrapping my arms around her waist. "You do?"

"Of course, I do." Clara kissed my forehead. "I've never been in a relationship before and I sure as hell have never done something like this."

"What? You don't have babies—" I shook my head. "I can't even finish my joke. Just the idea of another man touching you makes me want to gut someone."

"Yeah?" Clara placed a hard peck on my mouth. "This possessive thing you got going on here, is kind of hot."

A low growl escaped me.

She giggled, the sound sending shivers throughout every inch of my body.

"Oh and Ryder?" Clara ran her fingers through my hair.

"Yeah?" I sighed, loving the feeling of her touching me.

"I want to fall in love with you too."

EPILOGUE

Clara

EVERYONE WAS IN THE waiting room but all I could focus on at the moment, was pushing out this baby. My body felt like it was being torn limb from limb. Literally.

"Come on, Clara. You got this. You're doing so well. I'm so damn proud of you." Ryder's words gave me all the encouragement I needed.

After another push, followed by another scream with lots of tears, a loud wail finally filled the room. My body suddenly felt empty, exhaustion completely taking over.

"Congratulations, Mom and Dad. You have another son."

Tears rolled down my cheeks as our second son was placed in my arms.

Ryder wrapped his big body around me from behind, kissing my head, shoulders, and neck. He whispered how much he loved me and how much I made him proud.

"He's perfect," I whispered, my heart overflowing with love for my second boy.

"He is," Ryder said, his voice thick. "Just like his mama."

An hour later, I was resting on my side while Ryder walked back and forth, holding our son. We decided to name him Matthew. It was Ryder's dad's middle name.

Every time Ryder turned to face me, he gave me a smile. "I love you."

"I love you too." I faded in and out of sleep, wishing I could just go home and curl up with my boys.

For now, I watched as my husband greeted friends and family as they came into the room to meet the newest addition.

Angel handed me James, who was now two and a little man.

Ryder passed Matthew off to his mom and came up to me. He kissed me softly, letting his mouth roam down the length of my jaw. "Once you're completely healed, I'm making it a mission to fuck another baby into you. But until then, I'll be a gentleman."

"Aren't you sweet?" I laughed, shaking my head at my husband's mission to fill our house with kids.

"You think I'm kidding, baby?" He nipped my ear.

"You two need to keep your hands off of each other or else you'll get her pregnant before she even leaves the hospital," someone joked but I wasn't sure who said it. All I could focus on was the heat in Ryder's eyes and the promise laced in his words.

I cupped his cheek. "You want more babies?" I asked him even though I knew he did.

"I do." He kissed me hard on the mouth. "So rest up, Clara. We're going to have a lot of work cut out for us once the doctor's give the go-ahead."

I laughed. "Promise?"

He waggled his eyebrows. "Promise."

THE END

PROMISE US

The Next Generation Series:
https://www.aboutjmwalker.com/next-generation-series

ACKNOWLEDGEMENTS

Book 10. 10! I can't believe we are almost done this series. I wrote Grit, the first book in The King's Harlots Series, back in 2016. That series started off this world and now we're almost done the kids' books. To say I'm a mix of emotions is an understatement. I'm beyond excited to bring you all the books I have in my head but for now, we have one more book to release in TNGS. One more. *cue tears*

If you've read this far, I want to thank you. Thank you for reading my stories. Thank you for being part of this world. Thank you for taking the time out of your busy schedule to spend some time with my words.

My team: Angie, Christina, Jennifer and Joanne. I can't thank you enough for helping me fix these books up. Here's to bigger and darker stories ahead!

JM's Jems: You are my rocks. We may not chat every day and we may not have met, but each of you own a piece of my heart anyway.

Thank you to the authors, readers, bloggers, EVERYONE, who has shared my stories, cover reveals, read my books and so on. I can't thank you enough.

I hope you enjoyed this little freebie because book 11 is…well…you'll have to read to find out.

Happy reading!

xx

ABOUT

J.M. Walker, a Canadian author, is an Amazon bestselling author who also hit USA Today with Wanted: An Outlaw Anthology and the Dissent Anthology. She loves all things books, pigs and lip gloss. She is happily married to the man who inspires all of her Heroes and continues to make her weak in the knees every single day.

"Above all, be the HEROINE of your own life..." ~ Nora Ephron

Find me!

https://linktr.ee/authorjmwalker